No Brakes

No Brakes

A MODERN NOVELLA

Jakub Rucinski

JAMIE STANGROOM

Composed with men deprived of hope and chance in mind, anecdotes of boys left discarded and destitute. A keepsake, at last, of the indominable human spirit fully pushing against life's sore surges. To going over.

In memorandum of Galician war hero, major Józef Ruciński, who forfeited his independence to struggle for ours. Poetry echoes louder in Valhalla.
Dramatically dedicated to Troupe 6063.

No Brakes

Nathan told the men that the world was ending. He said they fed us trash since birth, that they sucked the passion out of life. Nathan's now in Reno, and I'm still in Carson City.

There's four walls around us, all grainy and bleached out, along with a reflective ceiling. My head is motionless on my shoulders, and the splashes of sweat from twenty sets of bicep curls still sit on top of my head an hour later. The beads of sweat drop down the little hair I still have and land on my bare chest, itself covered in blisters scratched by fingers almost skinned to the bone with calluses.

"The first step to ensuring a real tomorrow is sacrificing today," Nathan once told them, and my fingers hurt so much that I consider snapping them off, and the only part of my body I can still feel is my neck, and it's just because the sweat hasn't rubbed off on it yet. Once I drop my head down and stop looking at my own face on the ceiling mirror, the neck will become wet too, and I will feel like I've drowned. And they all left me, so I don't even feel like calling out names into the abyss. I don't feel like screaming, even though 'angry' wouldn't even begin to describe how I feel right now.

I am angry, yes. I'm furious, actually. At the corporatocracy at Harvin & Mille that instigated my layoff, at Duke University for rejecting my application, at my sixth grade math teacher for slapping my head on the desk, at Nathan, and especially at my father. I want to let go of all these things, to stop grasping at the little issues I have with everyday life. It becomes difficult when I'm not here, when I don't have this moment of temporary relief. But once I'm suffering, it gets easier.

This is what happens when you spend your days on a spartan diet. It's peppered beef and rice in the common room of the facility all day, every day. You wake up at five in the barracks with only one goal in mind: to harvest whatever you have of your energy, to push the physical limits of your body. You crawl out with the other men, and an hour feels like an eternity.

And once you feel like you're done being tortured, on Fridays, you come home, and the drive to freedom, a hundred and thirty miles for me to Sacramento, is the most satisfying, euphoric feeling you could imagine. Any moment your muscles are not being shredded and your mind is not dazed, and I mean really dazed, is a moment to be cherished.

And that's when you forget. It happens very gradually. You begin by forgetting your car keys, then the car itself, then your own name. Once you've forgotten who you are, you're a nobody. At Harvin & Mille, I was just a number in the system. Here, I'm not a number. I'm a *squad leader.*

When Nathan gets back, he'll have to look through the 'raw meat'. It's what he calls, and as a byproduct, what everyone else calls, the men who have not made recruit yet. They have learned the value of Nathan's work, whether they've been brought in by a member or had no other choice in coming (a common occurrence) but have yet to see the cruelty of this place.

They wear black coveralls and repeat phrases like "not all is lost", "pushing on", "gone over" and "war against the world" while Nathan eyes them and sometimes even nods. Inside the sweat room, we don't have any coveralls. We're all nude except for a pair of boxers, and it's now reaching two hundred degrees. The steam is getting in my eyes, and I'm finally forced to tilt my head down, albeit slowly.

Directly in front I see a bald head, but by peering out slightly further, I find another pane of glass. But this time, I can't see my own reflection dripping down on the floor. Instead, it's a translucent doorway, with a wall clock faintly revealing itself through the steam on the other side.

Devon, the man the bald head belongs to, could see it more clearly, but I know he has his eyes shut now to better handle the heat. He's thinking of his daughter in Queens who he hasn't seen in over a year. In fact, Devon has no idea where she is. But in his mind, she's right there with him, and the only boundary between Devon and his salvation is being able to get through this. That's also how he gets through the two-hundred pound bench press and four-mile run every day. He doesn't need to look at the clock.

If he did, he would see that we still have fifteen minutes left. I can see this because I'm a 'squad leader'. Only we can see the clocks.

The room was designed this way, you see. There are four grainy walls bleached out with white paint, the kitchen floor tiles below us that look as if they were ripped from a garage, a single window in the door and a reflective ceiling of glass. Devon is also a squad leader, so he sits in front of me, and both of us can see the glass pane. Our chairs are all the way to the right, and the right is right where the door is.

But there's also the left, and to both of our lefts, there are six men per squadron. If we look left, the sweat would fall in our eyes and rinse them open, until we were only able to see the responsibility that lay ahead with all these men. Responsibility, there's another word that Nathan would love. It's part of the four pillars of the Masculine Revolution. Along with Courage, Discipline and Ambition.

Courage. Discipline. Ambition. Responsibility is last in the usual order of things.

Before I can recite all four in my head, I impatiently glance at the clock once more. Fourteen minutes left. Time seems to pass us by slower every second, and even though I've been here many times before, my skin feels like it's melting now. These were no longer challenges compared to what the 'raw meat' have to face. Nathan refused to allow 'child's play' at any level after it. If you died here, that would be it.

No one's ever died during a task, not on my watch, but Devon has been here a year longer and he said it used to happen. I'm not sure I believe him. Then again, I have no reason to really distrust him. Not yet, at least. All people disappoint me eventually.

Devon has been here for a long time. When I was still a financial advisor at Harvin & Mille, he was already a big part of this place. Since then, though, not much has changed for him. One could even say Devon has become less relevant and needed. He hasn't lost hope, though. I think a part of Devon recognizes that Nathan knows he's found a way to get ahead, and that he, as our leader, simply has a way of figuring things out. But just in case it's a coincidence, Devon doesn't want to remind him. Maybe he will someday. Or, maybe he'll faint before he can.

Through the sound of coughs, jittering teeth and the deep groaning that accompanies the sizzling of the sauna, I can hear a noise of agony, one of those extended moans a man exudes before he passes out from heat exhaustion. I know it's coming from the back, several rows behind and to my left. Though if the truth be told, I have no clue who it might be. I've stopped keeping up with how everyone looks. There's always too many faces to look through. But I don't turn around to check. I try to set an example for my men. After all, I'm the only one of them who can see the clock, and I know we're supposed to be here until eleven. Somehow it's still ten forty-seven. Thirteen minutes left now.

I doze off and try to think about all the things Nathan could be doing in Reno right now. The men fighting for the Masculine Revolution, or at least the men who are supposed to, know some of his background, although often from an unidentifiable, miscellaneous source. I can't imagine Nathan thinking about the past at all, though.

He's always used the analogy about the Pirahã people of the Amazon rainforest, whose language doesn't have words for remarking on time, and who are therefore seemingly happier without the commodities of modernity, of which timed language is a part of, I guess. Once, Nathan even wanted us to burn the English dictionary. He told me I should know by now that too many words drive a society to insanity, that introversion is not real, that depression is caused by being stuck in the present and anxiety by living in the future. Nathan always swears he has a cure, even for the most abstract problems. But even when he refuses to acknowledge the past, I can't help but hang onto it.

I don't think Devon has quite forgotten the day he lost his daughter, even if in this moment, he can't recall his own name or where he lives. I think the sound of the judge issuing the verdict reverbs in his head like the ringing of bells by a church. For me, the audible memories are different. Ten fifty-three.

Sometimes it's the yelling of my father, but mostly it's memories of the girl who threw my life off-balance. Sometimes she's telling me, or a younger version of me, how we'll go to this place or the other, or what I should do or have done, or how it doesn't matter what I feel like, because the truth is *here* and the truth is *now*. Maybe she and Nathan had a spoken pact to bestow this realization upon all of us. Likely not.

Nathan grew up in the same suburb of Culver City as I did, and we both attended Yorksville High School around the turn of the century. But this is where our paths diverged, because he went to the Coast Guard while I went to university, albeit not the one I was originally heading for. My eager graduation from Yorksville was accompanied by a full cap and gown ceremony. Nathan did not attend.

I received a full-ride scholarship and was nearly drowning in opportunities, finding time to intern at various corporate finance groups around the country while learning in-the-field, and doing a student exchange in Costa Rica. The night I flew back to the Northeast, I got wasted and stayed over at my girlfriend's, Nathan got arrested for his third drunk driving infraction and was thrown into a Minnesota prison cell. Yorksville was not where we found one another. In the long term, it was more the globalism that bonded us, and globalism was not something Nathan was shy in speaking of.

He berated the world for being so connected in front of the 'revolutionaries'. He blamed modern technology and social media for killing the libido of men's souls and drowning out our sincere hopes. He wasn't incorrect in this assumption, but it didn't make it any less heartbreaking to hear. One would assume Nathan had an origin story, a reason for why he villainized the world and its traits the way he did, but the majority of us dismissed it, because he would never share.

Perhaps he did have a reason for starting the *cause*, but we would never learn it. You can pick up the pieces just as well as I can. The majority of the clues came from the way he looked. Well, when he was here in Carson City, that is.

A beige-brown jacket thrown over a white shirt, tattered combat boots, leathered dark crimson pants, a pair of sunglasses under his pitch black faded hair. All this with a furious, reddened face, the shape of which would put him in his late thirties or maybe early forties if not for all the scars. I knew he was thirty-five, though, since we graduated the same year. Nathan wouldn't have let himself get held back in school. At least, I don't think he would have. Ten fifty-seven.

When he stood in front Devon, he was an inch shorter, though he could make up for 'only' being six foot three with an impressive military-grade physique. When I first met Nathan at the bar, I was told by one of his eager observers, a girl who said she was studying biology at college, there was a rumor that he did three hundred push-ups each morning. I laughed and still find this comical, but for a different reason.

It used to be because I didn't believe it, had my arms crossed, was drunk and trying to get laid. It used to be because I didn't *know* Nathan. Now it's because I know he actually does six hundred.

Whether he changed his routine, or if it was because of a change in his supplement dosage, I don't know. But I've seen him do six hundred in the common room, just before we gathered in the sauna for the morning heat. Speaking of which, Devon opened his eyes. Ten fifty-nine. It was showtime. His hand raised at the same time the arrow on the clock struck eleven.

I wasn't confident in the uniformity. I assumed several things, among them that maybe Devon had a biological timer that operated silently in the background of his conscience, like *tick tick tick*. This could have been the case, or he could have just gotten lucky for the past several days, but he was always down to the minute. Truth be told, I was curious as to how he worked. I peered out, leaned in and looked at his face several times to see whether he was sweating just as much as I was. That's how I learned about the eye thing. It was during the meditation period that its meaning occurred to me, as if by superstition. Or maybe Devon told me. I'm afraid I don't actually remember.

Even if I did, it wouldn't do much justice in the moment, as we were on the move. Devon was the first to stand up, although wearily, and in several moments most of the men in his row were up. The one notable exception was Skinny Guy, whose real name is Slim, or at least that's what he told us. His lanky, pale body straightened itself out gradually, and his posture wasn't fully erect until all of the men in the first row followed Devon to the door. I stared at him menacingly, as did many of the men behind me. We couldn't leave until the first row was out.

Devon had to almost drag Slim out by his neck, and I could hear someone murmur in the corner of the room, likely agitated with the slowness, though only ten seconds had passed in reality. It was made worse when Devon's muscular arm finally lifted the hinge on the door, his flexor pushing against the glass pane and his hand wearily dragging it open, as if taking a deep breath. And then, it was my turn.

It was relieving to finally move my feet on the tiled floor. It was also relieving to feel my skin contrast with the flat surface. The sweat on top of my shoulders and head piled back down, sliding across my posterior, helping me feel the heat. As soon as this bucket of human water poured down my deltoids, leaving my back bare once more, my spine straightened out. I stood vertical, and took to moving my numb legs toward the door, hastening even more as excitement built within me. I heard a man sigh. My arm pushed on the handle, fingers scraping the hinge. I pushed *down*.

The room temperature of the common room hallway almost froze us to death. It was a gust of wind into an otherwise empty world, a hole in the fabric, as if opening a window into a vacuum on a spaceship.

As the cooler air hit my face, a conviction progressively mounted within me that it wasn't going to get any easier. For half an hour inside the sauna I felt like my skin was about to crawl off, as if I was trapped in an ant hill. I was, in my mind, on the beach with the sun revealed, the light burning marks on my body through an opaque roof. They began on the tips of my fingers and thawed slowly, letting the smoldering warmth run to the back of my hand. That cooled too, and now only my elbow was left to deal with the heat, escaping to the back of my arm. There it rested for a moment, until the man behind me, second in the row, approached through the door I pushed open.

I kept it wide to let as much air into the struggling men as possible. Now that I could feel each drop of sweat cool on my body, and my feet and legs became wet as if coming out of a shower rather than sizzling, my mind cooled off. It was no longer tugged by simple ideas, like the flickering ceiling lights above our bobbing heads, or the sound of our bare feet marching on the floor of the common room hallway. My mind now dealt entirely in complexities, in the abstract, the *abyss*. I couldn't let go of it as hard as I tried. All my words fell into it. I spoke nothing, but thought of everything, and especially the hardship of the moment.

Devon had now rested his dark, brown, rabid eyes upon Slim. His clenched, tanned jaw and the light facial hair around it, in contrast to a smooth head, gave way to an aggressive face, like that of a tiger about to jump at his prey. This was unusual, as Devon was not the type to hurry into confrontation. It was as if Slim, of the several men that walked in front of me, was the one who screwed up today. He was lucky Nathan wasn't here. Why was he in Reno, anyway?

Screwing up, like in the form of failing a challenge or breaking routine, was reprimanded in the simplest way possible: no food. The rare combo of extreme hunger and loss aversion prohibited the men from acting out of line. If there was nothing to eat, one had nothing to gain from all the struggle. A man exerting the utmost discipline upon his body must also exert it upon his soul. A soul without perspective is a soul without purpose, without reason. The heart and the mind grow into one. The heart and the mind *know this*. Ripped muscle cannot grow back without fuel. *Everyone* knows this. Even *I* know this, and you don't even know who I really am.

Have you ever seen a deer running through a swamp? A deer lost away from his fellow animals, the water around him bloated and sickly? There's no river or lake of freshwater for him to drink from, no bushes for him to eat. He's lost without a home, trailing a biome he likely won't return to, searching for a source of sustenance. Men, when deprived of necessities, act like animals.

Boys in school lunchrooms throw food around like stray dogs. The homeless beg for money on the street. And what about us? We needed water. Our bodies were falling apart because we were deprived of it, had little of it, were practically fainting. Even months of conditioning cannot prepare a man for dehydration to this extreme. I hadn't pissed in days, because every drop I drank was drained from me through exercise, and I only had a couple pounds of extra muscle on my triceps and abdomen to show for it all. It was about increasing the difficulty, preparing us for *anything*.

The twelve fountains, six on each side of the common room, immediately became filled with the first two rows. As more men arrived, we began taking turns on them. A blonde man with scars on his shin was so sweaty that he took off his pair of boxers and began wiping his face with it. Nobody paid much attention. Everybody just wanted to drink enough until they were sure they weren't going to die. Then they carefully backed away, wiped their face with their hand or a piece of cloth, or on one of the olive couches or futons.

This furniture, situated on the verdant green carpet, provided them with a retreat until the other men finished. Little time would pass until they too rushed to get another round of water, and this time, lean against the fountains, their lips almost touching the tip of the nozzle on the bubbler.

They were drinking from these machines as if baby deer from a tit. And this is the way this always was.

I wasn't one to lecture, because I was the first to take up one of the rightmost fountains, just a few steps away from Slim, whose lean leg appeared to shake in place. I questioned how he had enough stamina to keep himself on it. While doing this, I almost hit the bottom of my chin on the fountain. The entire interior had a Roman feel, albeit still somewhat trashy, as if a film set, which is something I just noticed now. I backed away. Today was sacrificed. A real tomorrow was ensured, but what about *next week*?

Really, I didn't drink that much water. Instead, I took prorupted gasping breaths while almost choking at the end of each long gulp. It was one or the other: drinking or recovering. In the moment, it felt like a journey, this one, was just about finished. At the same time, I didn't know what lay ahead. I knew there was something before me that day, something more sinister than an easy drive to Sacramento. But before I realized what it was, or maybe remembered, I was pushed onto the futon and remained there, catching gasps of the cool, cool, then warm air. The Masculine Revolution is still there inside me, and I blame some of it on Harvin & Mille.

Only a few of the men here knew Nathan, and nearly all of them had dropped onto the couches by now. Their legs trembled in place from the change of temperature, but not many were eager, or perhaps able, to get up and move. Each of them had something interesting about them.

Edwin, the man to my left, was a former Olympic runner in training, but the first thing anyone noticed about him was his long forehead. It stretched for what seemed like twice the length of the average frons, as long as the entire palm of his right hand, from the brows to the middle of his temple. Atop, a crew cut remained, now covered in sweat. He breathed heavily - I didn't.

The fountains were now empty, as several men had resorted to walking down the corridor once more to the room opposite the sauna, where the showers and lockers were. Some of them took out small bags, but not many had much in them. This would've been me had I not left most of my stuff behind at home, in my room. It would've been much smarter to bring some already filled bottles of water, or an ice pack, or at least a goddamn protein bar.

Recruits dispersed among the common room. Some Hispanic dude with long hair touched Slim's shoulder.

"Hey, Skinny Guy, be a little bit faster next time," his low voice reverberated throughout the room.

Slim didn't say anything to him, instead he just nodded his small head, albeit slowly, only lowering it a single inch before proceeding on his way. The comrade departed into the lockers.

In the background, the sound of cold showerheads began, accompanied largely by wild groans. I noticed, from the corner of my eye, the bulky participant at the far end of the room who was putting his pants back on, now wet with his brow sweat. I too had begun looking around, seeing what everyone had gotten to doing. As expected, some of the men went back to the clock, sort of inching away instinctively from the sauna, which they would not have the pleasure of being inside again today. Their heads were raised high, most were tall, and they attempted to look past the arms of one another onto the arrows of the clock. Five minutes had passed since eleven, and in another ten, the next period would begin.

This time of the day would scarcely be the easiest, as the next activity contained either a set of laps around the facility, done in a group, or an unusual variety of calisthenics training. Both were pioneered by a squadron leader named Neil, who worked alongside other men of the same rank as him and I to plan the activities of most days. Neil had been here slightly longer than I, but always appeared more engaged, energetic, with at least a few words to say. On lucky days, they would be sentences. Beyond the first week in here, speaking was sort of looked down upon. There were *very* few lucky days.

We didn't need to speak - language, on most days, came with the risk of saying something stupid. Once words were thrown out into the air, it was hard to make others forget them, especially in the quietness. Even men who on their usual days, in usual jobs, would display some sort of comradery with strangers or engage in lively chatter, would stay quiet here. The talkative flirt would shut up after just twenty push-ups, which was about how many Devon had done since falling to the floor in the hallway a moment ago. His eyes were once again closed, and several men passed by him and the showers to the gym room. A few 'routine men' left the pool room - their job for this period was cleaning. Our schedules were strictly organized.

One other reason we didn't need to speak is because everybody had sort of already been in the same situation. They had little to no home life and scarcely expected to get back to a stable environment, which always kept them on the go. They read the same books, believed in the same doctrines, and fully assimilated into the ideology. The marks on their skin were indicative enough of the price they have paid for inclusion into this avant-garde form of therapy. And most of all, they all had trust in Nathan, the ever-nonconformist rebel they imagined him to be. I wondered again why he was in Reno.

Moments ago I departed the sauna where I had just sweat my balls off, only sort of figuratively speaking. Now I was putting on the clothes that I shoved in lockers, retrieving my cargo pants, a white undershirt and my personal belongings. These consisted of my wallet, car keys and phone, which remained off. Before I could close the locker, though, I found myself on the go behind Neil, a six foot one man of exceptionally straight posture with a wet, white towel laid on his back. Edwin was running just behind me, alongside the other men in my row. While some were left behind in the common room to follow another set of exercises for the day, we departed down the hallway.

Near its end, where the 'exit' sign remained, we took a turn. The red lettering was a remnant of when this facility was a school, before it was a magazine, before it was Nathan's personal playground and our own place of rest. The turn led into a hallway passing to the right of the shower room, its ceiling removed along with the lights formerly embedded on it, leaving us in a dark passage below tangles of pipes up above. I really wanted to know what Nathan was doing in Reno.

The pipes made gurgling noises, but not for long. The passage had ended, and we found ourselves at another corner. What was formerly this middle school's gym was now the basketball court, a recreational centerpiece to this whole project, scarcely used except among the 'stayers'. This was what the men who spent weekends here were called, and weekends usually began on a Friday and ended on a Sunday. In those three days, the rest of us would work jobs or simply take a break. Some, like I, had enough money saved up to live like this for a long time. A bag of noodles cost ten dollars in Sacramento, meaning I scarcely spent over fifty in any given week.

Sacramento was what I thought of when doing laps around the court and its worn floor, perhaps constructed in the eighties, its architecture still beaming with the hopeful optimism reminiscent of the late twentieth century. I imagined the long drive home, the pile-ups on the highway, crossing the desert and smelling the grass. Then I imagined the stench, the filth, and the sloth of the city.

I heard the men behind me, my men, chant numbers. "One, four, seven, five," they sang, this seemingly random string of numbers accompanying them in their efforts. I thought little of it. It was still rather insane we grew up in the same era the Twin Towers stood proudly above New York. It was even more insane how the world has changed since.

The Revolution, Nathan said, would happen in a decade, maybe two decades' time, when he or his successor finds enough men. One man would land on Mars, the red planet, and illustrate the unlimited potential of human endeavor. This was when society could destroy itself, Nathan said, and we would build ourselves back up again.

But the vision of Mars ended exactly with the border of the basketball court, and after ten turns around its edges, or maybe nine (Neil never counted right), we made our way through another hallway down into a magazine. Another exit sign, another hallway, a window into the parking lot where some of our cars remained, a window into the future. Ten minutes had passed by the time we were in the common room, now emptied, and we didn't stop for water. The train continued again, and we kept on lapping around the facility. The men doing calisthenics would soon begin a period known as *study*.

Study was when we silently read books, albeit not the typical kind. Men under their squadron leaders had specifications. It was found, at a point unclear to me, that some men had humanistic inclinations, while others were strictly technical. At no point were we allowed to read fiction of any kind; novels, poetry and philosophy remained among the banned list, the only restriction to this being political books.

Nathan made it clear that politics only existed to cause trouble. In his words, they were the way to keep individuals fighting among one another to break intimate bonds, but at the same time, he strangely had no issue with entertaining this or that idea from time to time, as long as it remained radical. There was no clear affiliation, no clear tie to any set of beliefs, and one could go from one extreme to the other in a matter of minutes. And I still had no idea what Nathan was doing in Reno.

For example, Neil would sometimes describe how in our valiant efforts, we would need to work for one another from our ability according to our needs. The very next moment, he would extract his own cooled water bottle from a small azure bag, complete with a branded image, and explain how he believed it wasn't the duty of the squadron leaders to always keep themselves in check. Devon contrasted with this notion, although he never disagreed with Neil publicly, except at the squadron leader meetings, of which there was one every Monday. *Usually.*

No sick days, no days off. It was half until eleven and we were on our third lap. The second had taken a while longer, and for a reason unknown, we must have ran around the basketball court twenty times, from the end of the room where the bleachers once stood to the corner with the storage lockers. "Coal turns to diamond under pressure," the saying goes, and I must have been horseshit, because I really didn't feel like a diamond yet, so what else could I have been? Things just seemed to be getting worse and worse, all by the moment.

Two more laps passed and the feeling remained, albeit I felt myself getting somewhat closer to the end. This was until I saw Devon leaning by the water fountain. His eyes were fixated on something in the distance, but as soon as he saw me, he waved me in. I paid little attention at first, but his hand signals depicted it as being urgent.

"Recoil," I shouted, and the man behind me slowed down. This is the code word to stop in an emergency.

I fell back from the row to the side, like a truck switching lanes on a busy road, and Neil assumed leadership of my line. Our two rows now remained stacked with twelve men altogether.

Once I slowed my pace, I could see the worry on Devon's face did not fade. "What's the matter?" I inquired.

"You're going to Reno."

Something like a gulp was felt down the back of my throat, but it didn't remain there for long. I knew instantly something was the matter, and it was better not to object.

This was not my plan for the day, however. Something about the order of things getting all mixed up at the last minute made me frustrated. This wasn't something I was going to voice, though.

I nodded. "Is it important?" It was a stupid question, I know now.

"It must be," Devon said, his voice just as coarse as before, though unsurprisingly not mocking. "I can't expect that he's testing you, but if he is, you better get there quick."

"Let them know my goodbyes then," I solemnly admitted, eager to get on my way. A sigh came out, but I don't know when I let it.

I left the common room for the hallway, at the end of which remained the storage, through whose doors I could unlock the gate into the parking lot. Just as I made it halfway through the bust-out white door frame of the room, I looked back to find Devon's eyes still fixated on me. He didn't move an inch. "Yeah," I said, and smiled brightly, "I know."

Devon shook his head and crossed his arms. The bright ceiling lights of the common room illuminated the top of his head.

"For what it's worth, I hope you'll be back," he said. "You know it's all going to be worth it, right?"

"Yeah," I retorted quickly, "I know," although I wasn't very well sure that I really did.

The facility looked bleaker on the outside, especially from the parking lot perspective. The middle school had been scrapped twenty years ago, and I'm not sure whether anyone actually remembers the name of it. Nathan probably did, but for the rest of us, it was like a blur. The building, or rather the conglomerate of several buildings stretched out across this field, was sizable, but barren. The walls had been scrapped of stiles and their exterior ply, and atop the roof, no tiles remained. It was barren and flat from the outside.

It was an area that seemed somewhat desolate and removed from the outside world, although likely it was because the windows had been boarded up, locked away from the light gust of wind that blew by when I departed the storage. They had been covered in a way that did not seem lackluster or trashy, but precise and delicate. The aim of the four walls had, in the end, been fulfilled. Where there was a beginning, there was an end. The birthplace of what Nathan called the Revolution was in truth a low-end gym and library hidden in a compartment most similar to a magazine, but the parking lot was spacious.

There was enough space to fit the several trucks that stood toward the back, including a white GMC Sierra that cast a shadow upon the path that opened into the lot. Behind it were two smaller cars, a Mitsubishi Eclipse and a Nissan Quest, whose entire rightmost back window had been shattered. The other side of the chassis on the vehicle was also damaged, leaving the entire body of the car in a ruined state, as if it were hit from its side by a vehicle attempting to swerve in another direction. It was a miserable sight, and I quickly passed by to retrieve my own car.

There was a little patch of dirt at the end of the lot, next to it a curb, and parked by it my own Jeep Wrangler. It was a white car with a wheel shoved on the back of its body, low cargo volume, a strong tank and a body form proper to that of an SUV.

They say that a dog complements a man, it shows his character.

A feistier man will own a bulldog, while the owner of a golden retriever is hardly ever a nuisance to those around him, and will take up a much friendlier tone with strangers. I find the same is true with cars. It's not a matter of compensation, just an expression of character. The bigger the character, the bigger the car. I guess that said a lot about me.

Nevertheless, the pain of leaving behind my row of men, the discomfort, the smell of chlorine, was all catching up to me. For some reason I could not figure out, life felt more real on the inside, and I kept this thought with me as I unlocked the vehicle and started the engine. Immediately, the radio came on with a station blasting a hip-hop song I had never heard before. I quickly turned it down, drifting back into silence and falling back into the driver's seat. I tapped my finger on the armrest as the cool air began to surround me.

I could not handle this, either, as I felt the hypertrophy I had worked for fading from my muscles. It was, once again, like any other Thursday, otherwise a day where I'd be driving to Sacramento. The moment I got out of those doors, you see, the poisoned air of the outside world surrounded me. I felt disgust with commodities, with availability, with the ease of life so present here. The fact the air conditioning in my car was automatic meant that someone thought of it as an improvement, an advancement. A hundred years ago, you'd need a second person to fan you while you drove somewhere.

But there was no one to my right, nor to my left. I was free, but ultimately alone. It was a scary thought, even more so as you turn the knob on the air control panel, put your foot on the gas, and begin rolling away. There is no music to soothe you, just the sound of the gust of wind. After all that had happened on the inside, everything felt easier. The usual noise of the universe now fell on deaf ears. Nothing was intense to me.

Then again, it was hard for the intensity of the road ahead to kick in immediately, as the lot was situated nicely on the corner of Carson City. This meant that I was some twenty minutes away from the Nevada State Museum, and down the road from the suburbs was a supermarket, which usually remained busy this time of day, freeing up the road. Glancing at my phone, now placed atop my car panel, serving as the navigation system, I saw the time was in the afternoon, although I quickly forgot exactly what it was. This early in the day, I couldn't expect to see much movement anywhere.

Even if my brain were fried with thoughts, and my mind was several yards down the street at some point in the distant past or future, this wouldn't be difficult. At least that's what I thought, as I took my foot off the brake and stepped it on the pedal, before hearing a loud, clattering noise coming from down the street.

I quickly figured its source was in the form of a frustrated motorcyclist nearly missing the hood of my car, rushing down into the valley between greasewood and yucca trees, condensed in hotspots across the road. He descended down the motorway pathed in squares and rectangles and neatly falling down the hill into the town center. Seconds away from death and stopping me just short of leaving the parking lot, he lived on and continued wherever he was going.

The motorcyclist likely thought he had lived his life in the proper way. In his mind, I was a nuisance and he had been the one in charge of his direction. The boundless 'free will' he took for granted was a distant dream of mine, however. I don't remember the moment I finally made the right turn, and started driving in the same direction, eager to find myself on the road again. My pace was slow at first, but then I picked it up again. When I checked the time, it was twelve forty-five. I remember it now. I have to visit my girlfriend at the psych ward.

Driving through the northern suburbs of Carson City meant twisting around the edge of Lake Tahoe in the opposite direction to California. Since I grew up in Culver, I was only used to making this road driving on the other lane, so the journey began for me backwards.

As I pressed further down the road in the first five minutes, I could recognize this or that store, some stop signs, a gas station, but was convinced they were out of order. It was as if reality curled against itself, as if the biblical Heaven and Earth had at least been molded into one. For a moment, I was convinced that by the time I made it to the I-580, the road would lap around again, and I'd end up by the museum. Maybe that was just from all the running. I couldn't believe the goddamn state governor lived here.

On the sides of the road, in-between the overpriced leased plots of land and honking vehicles, remained small patches of dirt. Western hawksbeard and longleaf phlox were some of the flowers that grew here, reminiscent of when this part of the U.S. was still an oasis, a patch of a plains region stuck in the middle of a desert. Maybe before these lakes were drained of water and replaced with roads splitting off from the highway, birdnest wild buckwheat grew where the 7/11 now was. *Highly unlikely.*

They took the bushes of Utah junipers around Eagle Valley Viewpoint and made them into parking lots, a genocide of cacti ushering in an era of GameStops and Krogers. Parks of creosote and mesquite were demolished to make room for yet another Subway, while the public infrastructure crumbled below the pathways upon which ordinary men walked. And these ordinary men, lost in their purpose, would go through life as if it were a film they rented on a streaming service.

Humble beginnings amounted to a jobless father, a distracted mother and a mediocre high school. The Pareto principle applied, the masses were shoved down toward the bottom. One in five boys truly felt like they were living in their adolescence, one in five were not destroyed spiritually through puberty, one in five would never join Nathan's cause, my cause. No Child Left Behind limited classrooms to some twenty-two students, leaving behind two boys at most to command each and every group. This was the way we were conditioned.

Once they were adults, these boys would become bosses, managers, hanging above the shoulders of clerks, car wash operators and phone marketers. They were telling them they could work at Harvin & Mille with their cousin Clark if they tried hard enough. Even I had no right to complain, at any measure. The Pareto principle made the ordinary person into a stray dog.

Boys were rid of their souls so early now. We once had no desire to find ourselves in a better position. In the olden days, all of us would have been satisfied seeing our favorite musician or entrepreneur or other cocky extrovert driving a fast car down a stretch of highway on the television screen, while we were satisfied with a Jeep Wrangler, for instance. When we were kids, we believed we could be rock stars, senators and CEOs. Now Nathan gave us the understanding that someday we *would* do these things, only now we had to work in silence and put money away, walking towards something of a future one foot at a time, making everything of every step.

I thought about how I had enough to buy the crimson sports car that eagerly passed me by just now. I thought about how fast the bald, fifty-year-old man in it was going. There was no way he himself had enough money for it in his retirement fund, but maybe he wanted to live, if only just once in his life. I had to drive to Reno, and maybe if I survived I'd make it to Sacramento. Only God knew at this point, if even he.

As I took a turn by a fast food place onto I-580, from a distance I saw several teenagers returning from a swimming pool, an intrusive thought got the best of me, and I slowed down. The cars behind me began honking eagerly. I slept just four hours the previous night and had no clue where I would actually find Nathan, I just knew he was in Reno.

The map on my phone guided me toward some station I knew not the looks of. A car remained parked on the side of the road, an American flag waving it by, and I was being yelled at now for driving twenty miles an hour by someone with an open window. I was about to enter a goddamn highway.

Once I awoke from this momentary dissociation, I pushed half my foot on the gas pedal, accelerated to sixty in a matter of seconds, and almost smashed into the side of a school bus before changing lane. It was more terrifying that I didn't know if I would find Nathan in Reno than that I might not get there in the first place. I considered all the different possibilities.

I began driving at eighteen, although my father didn't teach me, because he spent most of his days at a cushy law office, and the little time he did have with us was not of great value. I say *us* to refer to my younger sister, Sara. She was still in Sacramento, albeit she didn't get a somewhat prestigious job like my former one at Harvin & Mille, despite having gotten into Duke. As much as it hurts to say, this was my only joy in life, along with the fact she couldn't drive, but if she could, I know exactly what it would be like.

There are several types of drivers, you see.

Ordinary Driver

Slows down before making a turn, rarely uses the horn, usually has music playing in the background.

Slow Driver

Refuses to push the pedal enough to accelerate to thirty miles per hour, will always let you pass by on a highway (or any fast lane), never misses a turn.

Self-Destructive Driver

Wants to get everywhere fast, does not care if it means their demise. Will speed up if you use your turn signal to indicate you want to switch to their lane. The most ironic of any type.

Divorce Driver

Will have a problem with anyone on the road slower or faster than them. If you're not keeping up with the divorce driver, you risk damaging your car. Will skip you.

I always imagined Sara as being something between an *ordinary* and *slow* driver, even though I've only seen her in the driver's seat of a vehicle once. That was when we were parked outside a supermarket, and I must have been twenty-six. In any case, it was a comforting thought, because I'd hate to be related to any of the other types, though I reasoned one of my uncles must have fit these descriptions. Even my father never put on his seatbelt.

The truth before me was that this list looped, and one driver could only crash into another adjacent to them on this list. The order here wasn't coincidental. A divorce driver can only collide with a self-destructionist or an ordinary driver. A slow driver will endanger these same two, strangely enough, but is not by any means above the divorce driver. The source of the naming will remain a mystery until the near-end of time, along with countless other things. And I still have to visit my girlfriend at the psych ward.

In any case, I now accelerated from sixty to seventy, and steadily moved along this pace on the I-580 fully knowing that with any accidental turn of the wheel, I could come spiraling to my death. Spending countless hours in Nathan's facility hasn't actually made me anxious. I guess a part of me has learned to embrace the possibility of death, of danger. But maybe another part hasn't matured - at all.

At that moment, I remember there is a radio in the car. I turn it back on again, but there's no longer a hip-hop beat in the background. The music is slow, tempered, and even though it's no more soothing than silence, it provides me with the same feeling. I decide to leave it on at a low volume, around as loud as the beating of the Wrangler's wheels on the highway.

It's strange to me, as I cannot make out the rhythm precisely, but it sounds around sixty beats per minute, and there is a loud saxophone solo in the background. It's not quite jazz, but something like a modernized version of it, eliciting the feeling of a theme from some movie I faintly remember, back when I still used to watch movies. I don't know which one. Probably something old and in black and white.

My gaze once more retreats toward the phone screen, I'm sure it's not good for me when the car's driving this fast, so I quickly revert my sight back to the road. By then, the truck that was driving in front of me has already been replaced by a Sedan. *I must be losing my goddamn mind.*

Driving continuously on the road for some time evokes a distant recollection that I'm not consciously aware of, something like a memory, but seemingly less real. I can tell it's from early childhood, but the exact timeframe is unknown to me. It becomes apparent to me at that moment how insane the prospect of not remembering the age one did something at is. You spend an entire year 'being' a certain number just to not associate it with anything.

How many wasted teenage years were spent just to not know when you first skipped school, or drank alcohol, or sneaked out with friends to the cinema? How many irrelevant memories and feelings of anger replaced the important human connections of the past, and how many friends were lost? I keep thinking sometimes to random strangers I've had conversations with on beach shores and atop mountains, years ago when I was somewhat alive. That was before I became a working drone. I keep thinking back to lost childhood friends and classmates and can't make out their faces. I don't remember their names.

This becomes especially true within the facility, I think to myself as my Wrangler continues to slow down. It's now dropping to a speed of fifty miles, several people thinking they're in a bigger rush switch lanes in response. My eyes skip the nearest exit from the highway, knowing I still have a long road ahead of me. My thoughts collect themselves, and I come up with an example. When I was dragging a set of dumbbells practically across the floor this morning, around four times heavier than what I used to lift just half a year ago, I felt great pain and exertion. Just several hours later, I feel the same as though I might not have even done it.

A man can survive wars, trek across the desert, experience countless romances and orgasms if he so pleases, betray friends and be betrayed, lose track of time and his entire life. At the end of the day, he will only look slightly different than he once did. At the end of the day, he might even feel the same way. As long as the primary needs are satisfied, as long as daily water and nutritional needs are met and there is a cushy place to sleep, which the green Earth has afforded us all, potentially up to ten billion of us, all is well.

Generations will continue as long as men are 'fine', I think to myself. But if men are just 'fine', they cease to become men. That would be Nathan's interpretation. There has to be some sort of morality, a greater meaning enveloped within the trail of life, even if it's nothing but our brains attempting to make reason of it all. At its core it's neither love nor faith, albeit both have provided me, at one time or another, with a feeling of belonging. It's the feeling of being itself, of helping, of serving a purpose. I had a purpose beyond the Masculine Revolution, and how many sleepless nights did I need to make myself certain of this?

I was still reluctant to call Nathan on the phone, as I rarely did, before coming to Reno. I still had some thirty minutes of road ahead of me, which seemingly wasn't a lot, but if I was walking and not driving, it would surely take me an entire day. Man being armed with bigger means he forgets the relativity of the world, how far apart everything really is. I too had forgotten how distant states, countries and continents were. I was born hundreds of miles from here, and yet here I am, hand on the wheel.

This hand now slides across to the right, as I suddenly make the rash decision to exit and refuel for gas, realizing taking the risk of doing so later, perhaps with Nathan in the car, would be a mistake. I could not guarantee he would not do something stupid, and so I had to halt him every way I could. I now believe my role in this movement has been one of moderation thus far, a rather nonchalant form of it. I was relied on for my logic. And so, I thought this as being the logical thing to do.

As soon as I slowed down on the exit from the highway, or rather, as soon as the Jeep did, the cars behind me began to come across as impatient. They were dissatisfied with how much time I was taking, albeit the entire purpose of the stretch of road out onto the crossroad ahead of us was to halt the speed.

There was only one lane, so I was doomed to speeding up until I almost tailed the car ahead of me, at which point the self-destructionist drivers behind me still didn't seem satisfied. I doubt they would've been satisfied if the windshield of my Jeep ended up halfway through the car ahead of me. The crash would've been too slow for them, the humble Earth not chaotic enough.

"It's getting too good, we're having too much fun," humanity says, "it's too easy to live, we can read anything, we can watch anything, we can talk to anyone, we can eat anything." Politicians shake their heads. "World peace is too boring," they admit in front of the United Nations, "we need oil wars, we need crisis, economic crashes, give us *something*, we haven't had a disaster in *so* long." Nathan is your disaster, and I'm coming to pick him up. But I had to get gas first.

The nearest gas station was, of course, just at the end of the crossroads. I drove by the lights just as they turned green, the jazzy music on the car radio now turning into the sound of a low keyboard piano and Frank Sinatra singing. I turned it down. I'm not quite sure I knew what song it was. I'm not too sure I really cared. And I still had to visit my girlfriend at the psych ward.

As I drove into the station, from the corner of my eye I saw several men in conversation, one wearing a black hoodie and the other a white sleeveless jacket over his similarly white shirt with some black numbers on it. The first one in black was bulkier, and some skinny-fat guy with large, oval glasses kept shouting "Tim! Tim! Tim! Tim!" from his left, clearly at him, but he didn't turn his head. I approached the gas pump from the right with the neon store light in front of me, Tim threw a backhanded slap to the other man's face, leaving his glasses without lenses and the frame then shattered across the floor.

The bloke didn't get up, and Tim returned to his conversation with the sleeveless man, who seemed entirely unfazed by this reaction. With the ceasing of annoyance, they now seemed focused on another startled man in brown, baggy clothes, who seemed like he was crawling toward the knocked-out guy in front of the store door.

Suddenly, when Tim looked at the man with a menacing side eye, the baggy-clothed guy stopped and sat back down on the ground. He had a medium-size store soda cup in one hand, and seemed to keep the other on the side of his left leg, which appeared faulty. Even he tripped upon it. As I got out of my car, I determined him to be somewhat of a local bum.

My eyes drifted away from him and to the gas pump, which I promptly interred into the car's fuel tank. When it fell into the hole and got attached by the hitch, I looked back toward the storefront, thinking it might be good to get something to eat. It was then when I saw the man on the ground staring back at me. When he finally caught sight of me, Tim and the jacket man left him be and walked away from the scene of the incident. I paid little attention and got out my wallet, read my name across the debit card, thinking of how blatantly short it was, and then swiped it across the payment bar. The gasoline began falling in.

Even though I already had a lot of gas in my Wrangler, these cars are particularly efficient because they are 1. Cheap and 2. Can fit a lot of fuel. With the soaring gas prices so often foreshadowed on the news, a political issue, one must know that the prices tomorrow, or even in a few hours, will be even higher. As such, one, a survivalist like myself, must take advantage of this issue, and fill up his tank to the extreme.

I am One. No, really, I am. It's a shame to place names upon people, assigned euphemisms and references by parents long gone. Nathan could've been named after his grandfather Nathan Sr., or some war hero, or someone from a film. In the end, no one really cared. The world continues spinning on its axis regardless of whether squadron leader One wants it to. And for any purpose, I could be you, or someone close to you, or someone cold and far and distant. It wouldn't make any difference to Tim, or the bum now crawling on the doormat of the store.

As soon as the machine detached and I switched the pump back into its spot, I eyed the homeless man silently, waiting for him to finally *leave* the storefront so that I could go inside. Hastily I reached for my car keys, locked it and left it in the distance, now becoming smaller as I looked back. Perspective is a funny thing.

As soon as I was inside the gas station I smelled the rot and disgust. Four-dollar soda cans, eight-fifty-five for a bottle of water, two hot dogs for six ninety-nine, five dollar pack of extra thin condoms with maximum endurance and stretchability. Cherry-flavored vapes, banana-flavored vapes, apple mango-flavored vapes, gasoline-flavored vapes, flesh-flavored vapes. Cards for online games, a set of plastic utensils, a store clerk who couldn't care less that I just opened the door and was already looking around for any given thing, a curly-haired, blonde teenage girl with her biker father, a little ring-a-ding-ding sound whenever someone came through the door.

Outdated cash register, an American flag in the corner, six-ninety-nine roasted chicken wings with eight hundred calories and a quarter of your daily protein. Chips, chips, so many different chips, the crunchy and the kale and the able. Veggie chips, vegan chips for the non-meat eaters, because growing muscle is a sin.

A QR code you can scan to rate this location and service. I'd scan it if I hadn't left my phone in the car. Nobody else had - they are all staring at theirs. Screen after screen, the television blasting and turned up all the way. I find out from it that we're at war with another Middle Eastern country as of yesterday, even though they were our faithful allies as of last year. The president is giving a State of the Union speech, and his shirt collar is off, his wife didn't tie his tie properly and is now smiling as he talks in softened language about what is essentially bombing children's hospitals.

At least one congressman speaks the language of that nation. At least one is in the president's party. At least one has to sacrifice his morals for what the president is now saying will be the "greater good". Is it really this late in the day? I look outside as I walk toward the beef jerky, the soda stand and protein bars. There is a small shelf of Italian sausages. I think about getting some and eating them later with cheese, if I'm still alive, but they're ten ninety-nine each. Ten dollars ninety-nine for a sausage. That's a day's worth of noodles, probably way more.

And there are no noodles, not here. Just chips - god, so many chips. And ice cream. Gone are the days of a mother or grandmother taking a little boy to the town for ice cream. Gone are the days of soft vanilla cream and chocolate chip. All of the ice cream bars are now packaged, processed, unable to be even put in bowls. The large ones are unfashiona-bleh, and the corporate CEOs above the common men had them stocked back into shelves. There is a mountain of trash somewhere filled with melted, expired ice cream tubs, ones that were good just moments before being thrown belly-up into the mud. Why does everybody eat this shit?

In the corner of the gas station, the girl who came with her biker father spills her blue slushie all over the ladder, and glances up toward me. There are no tissues around while he is checking out a wall of alcohol-free beer, and I can see the panic in her eyes as she finds herself unable to decide what to do.

Her face informs me that she is waiting to be yelled at for this accident, and quickly her expression turns from sugary indulgence to that of stress, probably induced by a string of past trauma. I stand there, unable to do anything, not enough time to do anything, not enough courage. She flinches when her father turns around, and at once, I hear angry shouting. I don't want him to shout at me either, because he reminds me of my father, and the girl of Sara. I ignore it, but I can't get rid of the guilt now. I'm supposed to be a grown man, aren't I?

There is little to no cigarettes or lighters to buy here, just a wall of vapes. I don't care because I don't smoke, but the absence of liquor actually does upset me, because I think of it somewhat as a staple of culture. Unlike everything here, from the Mountain Dew to the Dr. Pepper, people don't drink liquor because it's tasty. They do it because it hurts them.

It's the last form of salvation available to the common man. They raised the smoking age to twenty-one now, that's another thing I notice. Soon it will be illegal to slander brands. I, for one, am eager to submit to our new corporate overlords. Maybe someday people will be branded. Being someone's product saves me from the burden of choice. The ice cream doesn't have to choose, does it?

And neither does the eight dollar sixty-nine cent sandwich, which is what I end up choosing from the rack, just as soon as the shouting stops and I'm able to think clearly for myself, like any healthy adult should. I give the guy at the counter a ten dollar bill.

At this, he is clearly disappointed, largely because he *actually has to do his job this time.* He calculates everything in his head and gives me three dimes and a dollar back, but I'm not going to count the penny against him. They shouldn't be in circulation still, anyway. That, and I'm never going to see him again. At least it's improbable.

But as soon as I leave through the front door, and hear the *ring-a-ding-ding,* the homeless man is still there, and he speaks to me. "Hey," he begins lowly from my left, the first line of real conversation I've had in a while. He points at me and chuckles. "Hey, hey, you. You're the guy."

I wasn't going to pay him much attention at first, but now I'm curious.

I turn around and see the bum's worn, dark brown eyes. They're staring somewhere in the distance and have paused there, focused. He's clearly tired.

"What?" I ask. "Which guy?"

"What's your, uh, name?" he asks curiously, in an accent that sounds relatively Southern but not too distinct to guess where he's from. Definitely not Nevada.

I shake my head. "Not important. You said I'm the guy," I say and kneel down beside him, the sandwich still in my hand.

It is at this moment I regret not also purchasing a can of something to drink, but I'm too entranced by the conversation, which pauses for a moment. He gazes towards me, still lightly chuckling, but slightly more serious. "Do you know me from somewhere?" I ask.

"Yeah," he replies, monotonically. "Muh… Maybe."

I grow curious and look over to my left, where the fight occurred just moments before. The man, formerly wearing glasses, is now knocked out cold and unconscious. His beloved 'Tim', however, is nowhere in sight.

Instinctively, I let out a heavy sigh and look back toward him. "Do you know these guys?"

"No, I-" he pauses for a moment and begins coughing into his sleeve, as if choking on his words while shaking the cup in his hand.

"You what?" I ask, raising myself from the ground. He sits still.

His voice refracts from the pavement. "Don't," he murmurs. "Don't think so."

The conversation bores me. I begin walking away, eager to unlock the car and head in the direction of Reno once more, undisturbed, but he continues to follow me. I look back and see the biker and his daughter exit the store, and their eyes immediately befall the homeless man following me, rather than the heckler lying on the floor. From beyond the window I see the clerk for the last time, shoving a deck of Uno cards in its slot by the register and scribbling something on a sheet of paper, uncaring, apathetic.

Immediately before getting in the car I turn my shoulder and look back at the homeless man, just several feet away. He's almost treading now. "Where are… you headed?" he asks, a slow pause in the middle, the cup still shaking in his hand.

"Reno," I respond.

"Can I hi- hitch?"

And before I know it, a stranger who named himself as 'Joe from Georgia' is sitting in the back of my car as we head back on the highway toward Reno, way past Lake Tahoe and its nude beaches.

I'm going to leave him just a couple of blocks away before I call Nathan and figure out where he is.

That's the plan, anyway, as long as he doesn't barf in the backseat, which doesn't seem likely. As soon as we get on the road he begins hurling and holding his stomach in place, as if he's never been in a car before. From the looks of him, he probably never has, and his eyes remain fixated at some point in the distance. Obviously I didn't let him ride in the front seat.

It soon becomes evident to me that the road has already taken longer than expected. If I departed exactly when Devon told me I had to, I would already be in Reno. I assume all is fair for now, as not a single person has called me, but that didn't necessarily mean much. I still kept my navigation in the front of the car as I swerved onto the highway, hoping to complete my journey in less than another half hour, even with the traffic.

I'd depart off the I-580 in a turnaround and drive by Bakers Park, from which I would find myself in the Reno suburbs, with several Chinese places situated around me and the Reno and Tahoe International Airport, less grand than it sounds, in the far distance. Knowing Nathan, he probably would've gotten on a flight to Canada by now. I knew how restless he is. Jim from Georgia, if that even is his real name, keeps groaning in the back, although he has no real reason to. And I still have to visit my girlfriend at the psych ward.

The music is continually slow on the radio, albeit recognizable now. 'Fly Me to the Moon' plays softly in the background as someone I'd classify as a 'divorce driver' gradually speeds up in the adjacent lane, seeing that I'm not willing to take the lead. This pisses me off to a certain degree and I decide to push my foot on the pedal, enough to make Joe shake in place. His urge to vomit, assumingly from stress, does not get any better. "D- do you have a plastic bag?" he asks.

"No," I answer coldly.

After three or four minutes I want to feel the air on my chin, to see and smell the outside, so I open the window and begin peering out from the corner of my sight onto the highway. From the glass I observe the overpass of concrete stretched out as far as the horizon, where I can briefly make out a sign indicating that my efforts amounted in us getting to Reno accident-less.

A plane flies overhead, although at first it's a loud metallic hum to me. It reminds me of when I was a kid and would see them up above on family road trips, the kinds you stop going on once you grow older and firmer into adolescence. At a certain point, they're no longer of any interest to you. But when you're five, eight, or maybe even eleven, there's different perspectives you could take on them. Different ways to explore the world.

That was me during childhood, seeking different views of things. I perceived it as intriguing that from one corner of the room, all would look different than from another. If I stood outside a building, for instance, its inside would look almost cryptic to me. I'd walk around, not to a specific place, but just about everywhere, as if I was testing the barriers of the world within which I dwelled. And for some reason, even then, that world seemed immaterial to me. I know why now. I didn't before.

As I pull into the leftmost lane for easier departure onto the exit two miles from now, approximately into the road by Bakers Park, I grow the urge to throw all these memories away. The motto of courage, discipline, ambition and responsibility cannot come across as anything more than a catchphrase now, and I struggle to believe it was ever anything more. If the most revolutionary of movements cannot help but grow a brand image, are all of us fallible? Or maybe I'm thinking too deeply? Or maybe I wasn't gripping the steering wheel hard enough, or-

"Where you' goin?" Joe from Georgia's tone suddenly spawns an annoyed sentiment underneath it, as if I had done something wrong.

I'm confused. "We're off the exit now," I clarify, placing only half of my present attention toward the dilemma. "I'll drop you off shortly, and you can head wherever you're going."

"I ain't got no money."

My hand rests on the steering wheel and sweat runs down my brow. "I know that," I tell him.

A large, white GMC truck in the far distance, appearing somewhat similar, has an obnoxiously large bumper sticker. It says 'Big, Dangerous Dog' and depicts a pitbull, but it doesn't clarify where the dog is. Truth be told, *et in hoc tempore* I do not see one in the car. Frank Sinatra continues humming his harmony, and after a commercial interruption for an anti-aging cream continues into 'That's Life'. This is it, the end of the road.

As soon as we make it off the road, Joe begins to be a nuisance. "M-man, I ain't got no money. If you're gonna drive me, you're gonna need to drive me far-thar than *this*."

I begin to get annoyed, but attempt to reason with the man calmly. A part of me feels that I've already given this stranger enough patience. "Listen, *Joe*," I say, "I told you I was going to Reno, and this is where I have to let you out. I am here to visit a friend."

"Yar friend can wait. Can't you help?" Joe shouts from the backseat, the sickness now fading from his voice. He's gotten too comfortable.

"No, Joe," I reply, "he can't."

But even as I take a turn off the highway exit and onto the nearby supermarket parking lot, Joe refuses to move. "It's time to go," I tell him, "we're here." I park and turn the engine off in a distant spot.

"Thi- this isn't Reno."

That actually makes me laugh. "No," I say, covering my face with my hand, chuckling. I probably shouldn't be.

"This definitely is Reno, Joe. Now come on. I gave you a ride, I won't be taking you any further." I think my smile annoys him, but I plead anyway. "It's for your own good."

Gradually the smile falls from my face as Joe reaches into his already dirty, baggy clothes and pulls out a small handheld knife. At the realization that I not only let a stranger into my car but now upset him enough to possibly incite violence, I am fearful. At the realization of how motionless and useless my car is, and how far away I am from the supermarket door. I am powerless.

Although I try to remain calm, his hand is now shaking, and he holds the knife with clear intention below his chin. I start to panic. "What are you doing with that?" I ask. "Put that down," the words continue spewing out of my mouth. Five seconds of silence, then ten. The gradual stillness is upsetting me.

In a hasty move I reach for the car door, and he can see I am sweating all across the face as he groans. Self-named Joe from Georgia holds his stomach, but his faulty leg is still stable enough to let him hurl himself at the windshield of the car. He does this as soon as I'm able to put my hand around the door handle, narrowly missing his jump. I pull my leg out and scream before shutting the door almost in his face. "Shit, shit," the words come out of my mouth as I lock the car with him inside. My breath begins racing as I realize the sheer amount of things I left inside.

But alas, after Joe is able to pick himself up from the driver's seat, into which he seemingly shoved the blade of his knife, he lays motionless. The seat is torn into two separate pieces, and the unthinkable happens - the bum vomits.

His head lies still on my seat, and I'm left unable to figure out what to do. Now, in a way, his loose grip on the knife comforts me as I observe it through the windshield. It's a sensation almost as if I missed a bite from a stray dog only to watch him get stuck in a fence, between iron bars. If only he were smarter, he could unlock it.

The sudden act of aggression shows me just how foolish I was to let this stranger into my vehicle. Joe's pale, scratched face remains upside down and sickly. I can hear a few long, hard coughs from inside of the car. Whatever empathy I had for this man, is now long gone.

Cleaning up the scene was a somewhat challenging endeavor, albeit it took less time than expected, and I was still glad to have survived. Joe from Georgia, however, which I'm by now convinced was not a real identity, was thrown out onto the pavement. After having him hold his rib and howl in what I assumed was a sudden yet non-serious inflammation, timing decided by the heavens themselves, I viewed him as harmless. It was then when I took off his second shirt and began wiping the puke off my dashboard, passenger seat and floor.

When it was done, I threw it back at him. Joe managed to sit himself upright, although shaking, and muttering something. Of all the things near us that were lying around this parking lot, he picked the vomit-covered shirt up and sat on it. I didn't feel like saying much, because I still had to sit in a seat that fell several inches below due to the tears, and almost couldn't see the windshield of my own car. Just inches away were my keys, and I used them to start the ignition. When the door shut, I felt like I was five foot six again.

I quickly drove away, and by the time the Jeep Wrangler reached the storefront, there was a man with a large cardboard sign saying "I Need A Ride". He was waving it around frantically, even at the face of a boy on a bike passing by. What was he going to do, jump on his back? I almost felt like picking the man up in the now-clean passenger seat, driving down the street and showing him what happened last time, why he wasn't getting any luck, and why people couldn't trust strangers nowadays. I almost did. But I had to pick up Nathan, and that was still my priority.

Determining that I'd fulfilled my promise of dropping the homeless man off, I reasoned that Nathan couldn't be far from here. Albeit something of an hour and fifteen minutes had already passed, and even though I was much further behind schedule than anyone else would be, I was still here. I reflected on my actions while making the turn, hopeful to park on a street corner.

Did I act with courage? Most certainly. Discipline and ambition? Not really. Responsibility? Hell no. But I doubted whether anyone at the facility really cared. I just wanted to get back home to Sacramento. My eyes were already dozing off in the distance from sleep deprivation.

I finally called Nathan on a street corner just outside a bike store. Pedestrians kept passing me by, each of them dressed somewhat like a person I'd already met before, or even knew intimately. The ringing of the phone began to get on my nerves, and I remembered to shut off the music in the background completely. For the first time since the confrontation with Joe from Georgia, the sweat began to spiral down my brow again.

And then the line connected. "Well, well," said the captivating, somewhat brittle voice that emerged from the other end. "Is it the designated driver this time?"

"Nathan," I paused, "where are you? I'm in Reno, by thirty-first avenue," the numbers came from memory.

There was a small silence. "Where by thirty-first avenue? No, don't tell me. You got a new car," Nathan said.

"I haven't get a new car," I explained. Nathan had never been inside this one, so I'm not particularly sure why he would care.

"Are you near any stores?", I asked.

"Only one selling overpriced German fixtures and appliances," he told me.

I didn't find this too amusing after everything that had happened to me, but decided to disclose to Nathan that I'd make a few turns and be right there. "Wait at the front, near the disabled parking spots," I elaborated, getting the visual in my mind. The line stopped for a moment, and I only heard a distant, croaky and low voice. "Okay..."

Then we disconnected. I took a heavy breath and closed my eyes for a moment, attempting to find myself amid the chaos. The fear that something might immediately go wrong kicked in once again, as it had many times before. Although a part of me believed I wasn't brave enough to handle him in the car, another tried to drown this thought out to set aside the fear. I thought of pausing for a moment, remaining still to calm my breath until I forgot all about these worries. Unfortunately, though, I didn't have enough time to do so.

Nathan was waiting by, or more accurately walking around the middle of, the three disabled parking spots by the large furniture store, some two hundred feet from where I was originally parked. Considering just how large of a city Reno was, and how much he must've moved around in talking to his many contacts, seeking all different sorts of stimulation, I felt this a lucky coincidence.

All my doubt in being late disappeared, as it truly appeared to have paid off the moment I circled the parking space and honked my horn. Nathan looked up immediately, his face devoid of any sort of anger, and an appearance that would be difficult to forget from then on. He wore a pin-striped white shirt below a corduroy collar-patched leather jacket, with a black button and one pocket sewn onto the left side. This and the jeans appeared to be dirtied in something like mud, which I only realized as Nathan approached the car, and unlocked the vehicle.

"Hope you've enjoyed your stay," Nathan said as he threw the seatbelt to the side and put his feet up on the dashboard.

I groaned. "My stay where?"

At first, Nathan cast me an almost intimidating glance, but he quickly smiled. "Well, at the biggest little city in the world," he explained. "Took you a while. We're going back to Carson City."

I started the engine, still tired and seemingly unfazed. I was reluctant to make conversation in the first place, and it appeared somewhat strange to me that the eager conversationalist was the one leading us. After all, the Masculine Revolution was a predominantly reserved group of silent workers and bodybuilders. We must have seemed like an ant farm from the angle he was looking at.

Nathan almost immediately spotted my reluctance, and began glancing at my face as I drove out of the parking lot. With the traffic around us, I thought of catching his eye contact and explaining my theory of all the different kinds of drivers. Instead, however, I wondered how long it would take for him to say something if I chose to say nothing at all.

After two minutes, he finally stopped looking at me after realizing I was attempting to appear entirely focused on the road. The moment he glanced at the rear-view mirror, I looked at Nathan's back, and noticed that this side of his jacket was scratched all over, as if he had fallen into some kind of pit.

I couldn't help but ask. "Something happened?"

He seemed genuinely surprised at my change of attitude, but quickly relaxed. "Yeah, squadron leader. A lot happened." His eyes peered toward the bottom of my stained seat, which I only now realize he must have noticed. "I see the same has been true for you."

"That's been there forever," I expounded.

This is when Nathan laughed. "Sure it has," he says, fingers retreating into his pocket to find a cigarette. "Do you smoke yet?"

I shook my head and admitted a 'no'.

"Tough luck," he said, lighting the cancer stick as soon as it entered his mouth. "Smoking is exercise for the brain," he said with the cigarette between his teeth.

"I thought that was reading," I propose back, turning onto the I-580 to make the same route all over again.

He began laughing, loudly, small chuckles turning into a daze. As soon as Nathan took the first puff of the cigarette, his mood seemed to lighten up. It was almost as if he was seeking the most difficult of habits. "It's bold," he said, "you're the *only* one who can stand up to me."

"I'm just the only one that's willing to," I said, locking my eyes on him as the car sped up. My gaze fell on Nathan's pin-striped shirt for a moment, and then back to his face, covered in full with facial hair and wedged around the cheeks. "I'm the only one that knows you, Nathan."

Nathan chuckled and took out his wallet. "Why don't you let me drive, huh?" he asked. Another moment of silence befell us, as he pulled his license out of the small compartment inside of the slip. I could make a brief distinction.

The words at the top were evidently clear in the afternoon, Nevada sunlight that was now peering out through the windshield. 'Nathan López' the identification read, with a date of birth in the late eighties as I already knew.

My vivid memory, even in the exhaustion of the drive, caught that he had scribbled out his address with a marker, and the card had expired in May.

"Huh?" he asked. "I can drive too, you know," Nathan said, returning the card to its original slot.

"Nathan," I calmly explained, switching the lane to the middle. "Your driver's license is expired. Not only that, it's damaged. You might as well have the corner cut off."

"When's the last time anyone checked your driver's license?" he asked.

I thought for a moment. "When's the last time someone checked yours?"

And that's when he started chuckling to himself again, although his voice now assumed a rougher tone. "Good call," he joked, "Wow, you're a smart guy."

My hand remained on the steering wheel, the fingers shaking. I was almost anxious, almost, to ask the important questions I knew I had to get out. Dawning upon me was the realization, however, that even if I did ask them, even if they did make sense, I probably wouldn't get a clear response.

In the daze of the situation, I went through with it, only because I had gotten this far. The future was uncertain, after all, especially with a divorce driver in a Ferrari speeding up to my right. "Are we going to be scrapping the humanistic studies?" I asked him, in relation to the books still at the facility of the Masculine Revolution.

"If the second house votes on it, yes," he replied.

But this only had me more confused. "What second house?"

Nathan groaned, and I felt a rant coming on. "Don't you know by now that I don't go places simply to catch a break? I had my purposes in being here. The first facility was financed, on a loan. We managed to convince the bank to let us off, and we're there for now, but not forever. We have to expand, to grow."

"What do you even mean by that?"

"It means that money is an issue," he resumed. "We have to resort to different means now. There's a school of a hundred and fifty men, yes, a hundred and fifty now. That's in Carson City, where we're heading now. And they do better with Neil and Devon and you in charge than they do with me, do you understand?"

My hand remained on the wheel, and I wished I had Frank Sinatra on again, because at least the music was sweet. We passed by another exit, and a distracted driver swerved in the right moment off to it, almost ending up as a decoration on the pavement. "So what," I asked, "you're making another Masculine Revolution?"

"It's a name!" he shouted. Nathan seemed anxious now, kicking his feet in the passenger seat. "The Masculine Revolution remains the same. But you can't stay in one spot. Ask Stalin."

"He's dead," I retorted. "You're seriously quoting Stalin now, Nathan? You bought a flat and negotiated with the banks, and you're quoting a Soviet leader?"

The voice I eluded seemed more monotone than mocking by now.

"Do you believe that we have a cause here? That there's a purpose? That we could do without the humanistic studies, without reading papers written by people outside our circle?"

"I guess so, yeah," I said as I held the wheel.

Nathan shook his head. "Don't guess." He seemed disappointed. "Man, you're my number one pioneer. I was eager to get you down here, you know why? Because even though you're late, you're trustworthy. Any other man would've left by now, and yet you criticize me freely. It's amazing, I could never do that. It's why I see you as my successor."

"As your successor?" I asked, reflecting on the children of Ares, still running laps and lifting weights across the rooms of the former middle school. We got closer to them by the mile. I couldn't imagine telling the men in there what to do, each and every step of the way.

"Yes!" Nathan answered back. "I mean, really, who else could lead us to Mars?"

I took a moment to take this in. "So that's the end goal of it all?" I asked while collecting my thoughts. "Wear them down, build discipline and loyalty…"

"And ambition, and courage, and responsibility," Nathan added.

"Yes, *that*," I said, "and then we go to Mars?"

"Well, first, we need to burn it all down."

I couldn't keep up with his train of thought. "What?" I questioned.

My passenger groaned, taking a loud cough. He stretched out his hands as if about to explain something grand, less an idea and more of an intricate concept. "Let me ask you this," said Nathan, taking up a strange, philosophical mannerism of a professor. "What year are we in?"

I told him the year.

"That's correct, and we're in *anno domini*, right? This is the year of our lord, supposedly?"

I still couldn't disagree, "Supposedly, yes." Although I regretted that this might turn into somewhat of a religious debate.

I couldn't tell where Nathan was going with his rant. We were driving at seventy miles per hour, and I had to visit my girlfriend, Amanda, in the psych ward, and was wondering what I'd be doing at Harvin & Mille at this moment if I hadn't been laid off, or if I could be a Duke graduate like my sister. In the end, all of this remained pointless.

"Listen," Nathan said. "That year you just said?"

"Yeah?"

He made a popping noise with his mouth, almost as if chewing gum. "Irrelevant!" he shouted, as the cigarette fell out of his mouth. It left a small burn on his shirt and then died, slowly, but he brushed it away as if nothing happened. "They didn't even calculate the years properly. Was Christ born in December of the first year, or the year before? Why isn't New Year's on Christmas? Are we doing it right, or are we using an outdated system?"

"I never really thought about it, Nathan," I freely admitted. I just wanted to know whether we could still read Dale Carnegie in Carson City in between our squats. I couldn't tell him that, though. He was already excited.

"So that's what I'm saying," he said. "Burn it all down. Who cares who gets hurt? Not to diminish it all, but this second house will take up a greater role than we ever will in Carson. This was just the start, my friend."

Nathan pointed at my phone, showing the road ahead of us. "That's helpful now, sure, but the moment the cars on the road stop working, we won't have any use for it. We won't need to know what time in the afternoon it is, just live like our ancestors did. When the sun's up, we hunt. When it's down, we sleep. It's the natural course of things."

"So what are you saying?" I questioned in scared intrigue.

"There's too much history," he said. "Too many wars fought to learn about, too many books written, too many films made and music to listen to. We cluttered it all, it's infesting our minds."

Up to that point, I could agree. Nathan coughed. "Listen," he said, "don't you think twelve years in school is a bit too much? They send little six-year-olds in there and by the time you're done, you're a legal adult and already depressed?"

"I mean, yeah," I said, albeit I was always somewhat of an honorary student. Not a valedictorian, by all accounts, but at least something relatively close. My only ever dip in grades occurred in sixth grade, truly, and was punished and reprimanded greatly.

"Yeah!" Nathan yelled. "Listen, when you throw all the stuff out of your room, the world becomes simpler. You can focus on your work, the things ahead of you. You don't return to the past, not even by force. What's the point of teaching everybody history if we're all bound to forget it?" He groaned. "Burn it down, burn it *all* down. The books, the phones, archives, catalogs, every product manufactured since we made the first factory stand still. Humanity lived before it all, and we will outlast it."

I was too tired to remember everything he was saying, but the prospect of it all still scared me. The sweat that poured down my arm touched my fingers, sprained and red from all the exercise. "So we restart it all? To year zero?"

"Look at your arm, man," Nathan said, pointing at my biceps. Muscle had grown all the way from my wrists to the trapezoid, and even my hands were beginning to look strong and bony. "Do you know how many logs of wood you could lift? You have no need for *this*, this car, this phone right here. You've benefited. Don't you want a future where no one, except your own tribe, can outrace you?"

"I'm not sure," I answered.

It was at that moment when my hand began to hover over the steering wheel that I first began losing consciousness. The sheer extent of the I-580 ahead of us made me somewhat dizzy, and seeing the cars around us pace to their destinations as I turned my head in this or that direction didn't help the tiredness I felt, the exhaustion.

My body didn't want to be awake and touching a machine this large, determining my own fate. I heard a large, metallic hum, and my last glimpse of Nathan was his face. It was determined. Virile. "It's the end of the road, man," he said. "Gone over."

I woke up in the hospital in Carson City. There were several nurses gathering around me, and one told me to sit upright just as soon as I regained some of my sanity. I was asked if I had any pain in the shoulders and lower back, and I said I had some, but most of it was in my hands and arms. They asked if it was from the crash, and I said no, and that it was there before. Confusion arose.

Sara was the first to visit me later that day, saying that they didn't allow any visitors in the first twenty-four hours, or she would've come sooner. The moment she arrived with her long black bangs settling over her freckled face, she almost started crying.

Apparently dad argued that it was all my fault, that he wasn't going to have a son who can't drive. This started an argument between the two, but she seemed relatively fine, albeit emotional. Once the first tears stopped pouring down her face, she seemed somewhat relieved to be here with me.

"They thought you were trying to end it all at first," she said. "Your car was all torn up from the inside, so they said if you had severe injuries, they wouldn't be fixable." Sara paused. "The doctor said you almost went into a coma. And… And Amanda said she would've come when she found out, but clearly… she can't."

"Water," I responded. I blinked suddenly with my head still in restraints, as Sara handed me a small glass. I began gulping it down, and it hurt every time I swallowed.

"I guess what I'm asking is," she paused, "are you okay?"

"What happened," my mind queried, "to Nathan?"

The stress of seeing Sara look down to the floor below her plaid white shirt and jeans told me enough. She wasn't in the mood to talk about it, but was quickly excused by several police officers. Before she exited the room, she smiled. "It's going to be okay," she told me. "You always find a way."

I was glad, partially, that the police confronted me about my case, mostly because of Joe from Georgia, who I otherwise wouldn't have told anyone about. I wasn't able to tell them much, though. They asked several questions, including my name, but I could only answer with a murmur. My throat really hurt.

First, I said to one of the two officers to turn off the television. The overweight presenter on it was talking about some NFL team I didn't know existed, and I was too tired to reach for the remote. He did as I told him, and I felt my authority as a taxpayer for the first time in this miserable life.

The officers were eager to throw presumptions at me, and it was clear they were trying to play 'good cop, bad cop,' which really bothered me. My sudden recognition of their methods was mostly because I used to watch too much television. I could tell they did, too, as they looked as if they were moments away from leaving to get donuts.

This would be my break, though. At long last, I was the show of the entire hospital, otherwise filled with appendix removals, broken limbs of construction workers and teenage girls with eating disorders. I wasn't going to tell them about the Masculine Revolution, because first of all I wanted to know if it was even still on.

Before the end of the conversation with Nathan I assumed that I was their new leader. Not because Nathan was dead or anything. The delivery truck behind collided with us rapidly from the left side, bouncing my Jeep off to the side of the highway where it flipped upside down against the concrete. At least, this is what I was told.

I didn't remember any of it, though. Apparently Nathan, the temple of muscle that he was, found himself able to crawl out, although badly beaten. They were now dealing with the burns on his face.

I was told how lucky I was to have worn my seatbelt and gotten insurance, both of which I thought were a waste until now. I felt like a cat being pet, grateful for the attention I've been given. God knew over the past few months I'd gotten very little, except maybe from the targeted messaging in the media. They said they'd try to find out who Joe really was, too, which was reassuring to a degree. Maybe I'd figure out the mystery, although to what satisfaction for myself, I couldn't tell.

One of the officers smiled at me when I told him I hadn't been affected. He would've liked to be a squadron leader, too, I could tell. Too bad he only came to the meetings on Mondays.

When the other, much less flexible cop left the room, eager to call his wife on the phone, it was just my friend from the facility and I. It was difficult for me to complain about his absences. I wasn't a stayer, anyway.

"I saw the scars on his face," Jeremiah finally said, still wearing the outfit of a police officer. He blended into the role perfectly. "Even if Nathan gets out, he won't make it long with us in person. It's really bad. His cheeks are flattened, he hurls all around the room, the pain has caught up with him."

I coughed into my arm. "Wouldn't that just help him, though?" I said, tiredly, my eyes still fixed on the glass of water.

The improv cop shook his head. "Not when it's this bad."

I looked shyly again toward the drink that Sara gave me, that the blonde nurse was about to take away. Feminine compassion seemed miles distant. The water, only a few yards. The door closed. Me and Jeremiah were alone again.

"Listen, when you come back," Jeremiah said, "and I trust you will, enough about Mars. Enough about sons of Ares, the four principles, toughening our souls and spirits. We don't want to burn the world, just catch a break from our lives. Neil feels the same way, I know he does."

I paused. "We're all just searching for meaning."

"Don't let it get lost in the abstract," he said, raising himself from the hospital bed. "Your body's already worn out. If your mind goes insane, too, we'll lose you forever."

"I'll keep myself sane," I smiled.

He lifted the handle on the door, then looked back at me. Tall and fibrously built, for the lack of better words, Jeremiah looked like the most healthy hedonist of this generation. He smiled back for the last time, resting his hand on the police cap. "Order a pizza, or something. God knows you have enough money."

"God knows *everything*," I murmured to myself. The door closed.

I sneaked out at night that weekend and visited Sacramento by rideshare, albeit my phone, complete with the cracked screen the weightier police officer warned me of, remained almost unusable. Seeing the sun set across the evening sky in the backseat of the vehicle filled me with a sense of calmness. It was resonance, it was conclusion, it was the warmth of the sun and the parents who never bothered to show up.

It felt strange, the thought of entering the mental health facility in patient clothes. I was afraid they'd mistake me for someone, and lock me up for good. Being deprived of my freedom again wasn't on my bucket list.

I made sure to stop by a department store along the way. As I was trying on a light blue flannel in the dressing room, the first piece of clothing I bought in months, I tipped the driver through the app, and then turned my phone off again.

Ambling out of the store in this new style, I was uncomfortable wearing brown chinos, but happy to leave the patient attire in the back. I wasn't going to return to the hospital, even if Sara insisted, as I'm sure she would. Fifteen unanswered calls, seven voicemails. I was ignoring more people than a college girl by now.

I'd need to turn my phone on again to confirm my identity via my emergency contact to the nurse at the clinic, who was doubtful of my I.D. picture without any bruises, but this wasn't much of a bother now. I already felt like I was living in a dream sequence, the way you feel walking down a road while dazed in the middle of the night. I appeared more cheerful now, although I couldn't tell why. I was just as powerless and miserable as before, but maybe with an overwhelming sense of relief.

After arguing for ten or fifteen minutes as to why I should be allowed to visit my afflicted partner, the nurse relented and let me down the hallway. It wasn't until she told me to wait by the wall that a doctor, tanned and in a white lab coat, informed me that they had to wake Amanda up first, which made me feel bad.

I would've told the nurse I could sleep in the waiting room until morning. I was tired enough to. She didn't say anything then, though, or maybe she did, and I just forgot. It was all scarcely relevant now. Either way, I was doubtful Amanda would show up to see me. It came as a surprise when the nurse returned and told me to wait inside the visiting room while my girlfriend changed.

At that moment, I wondered when I would die. I wondered whether in the instance I see my death, I would ponder upon my life and its miniscule details. It would be, likely, through the eyes of another car crash, old age, a sickness or the aggression of another Joe of Georgia once my foolish empathy returned. I could not tell yet, even though I was a predeterminist at heart.

Free will could be nothing but an illusion, after all, but this is the issue I always liked most in existentialism. Could I factually be mad at anyone that upset me in my journey, when in their shoes I would find myself acting in the same exact way? If I thought like Nathan, was brought up like Nathan, and was treated like Nathan, I would be Nathan, wouldn't I?

And because each step in Nathan's life led to another, and each step in others' lives led to Nathan's, there was only one way things could have worked out, wasn't there? I mean, really?

If our souls are an abstract concept, and the body I trained for so long is the only thing that really remains, then things were always meant to be the way they turned out. This scares people, but for an unknown reason to me. I do find it comforting, because, it's like, kind of knowing how your favorite movie will end. Ironically, the moviegoers dislike this perspective. I scarcely talk with them anyway, though.

Everything was planned and ahead of me, and I could not see it yet, but my legacy in this world would live on through the memory of others. It was because records existed, because history was written, because books and journals were made by other persons than I that the world could live on. If our ancestors knew we'd bury their memory in the ground, they never would've allowed us to come around in the first place. It is our duty, then, to maintain their memory. I wish Nathan could've seen this. Maybe someday I'll tell him.

I questioned whether the day I die and end up on the stairway to heaven, I would fall like one does in a dream, fighting for their conscience. I could wake up in a sudden moment, maybe for a minute in a hospital in Carson City or Reno or Sacramento, where I was now, and murmur something to the doctors. Then I'd forget all about it and become mortal once again, fading from life, but my memory would live on in others. Sleeping, a form of death rehearsal, prepared me for this all my life. I was ready to finally go. Me and the Queen of England were at last equals in the human experience. Me and all the figures of history.

But God would treat me indifferently, and the conversation would go somewhat like this. "Gone over."

I'm on a road with no breaks, there is no end in sight. I'm about to go over, aren't I? It sure feels like it…

I would stop at the entry to the heavens, where His Son would decide whether to let me stay here, or become the emperor of purgatory, a title I feel deserved. We would talk, and Christ would question what exactly happened, how I got to this point, and I'd ask him. Did I make it past the mark? Did I go over?

"You were hanging on the edge of a cliff, my son," I would be told, but not by my earthly father, but by the universe's own maker, the glory and fear of which I know not and don't wish to know in my life here. "It was very steep," I would be told Jand see, "and you were seconds away from falling, but your arm grabbed on to the edge. And just like the figures of history, you'd gone over. Gone over like the Frenchmen at Waterloo, gone over like Alan Turing in his creative genius, gone over like any hero living a hero's tale."

"Was I a bad person, father?" I'd ask him.

"No," his wisdom would say, "you were simply victim of a world gone insane."

Gone over. But the world will keep spinning.